www.carameltree.com

The Brainstormer

CARAMEL TREE

Chapter 1
An Ordinary Boy

There was nothing special about Jimmy. He was just an ordinary boy who lived with ordinary parents in an ordinary house. You could see a boy like Jimmy anywhere on the streets. Well, maybe not *anywhere,* but you could still find someone like him, if only you could notice him.

It was a little hard to notice Jimmy. He didn't talk a lot. At school, he didn't talk at all! You probably wouldn't notice him even if he was sitting right next to you. The children at Jimmy's school certainly didn't notice him much. The only times they heard his name being called were after the school tests.

The teacher, Miss Gwen, always called Jimmy's name after each test because **Jimmy always got a perfect score.** He was the cleverest kid in the whole school.

Jimmy didn't have to study very hard. His head did all the work for him. His head seemed to absorb everything that was being taught at school. Everything Jimmy had ever learned was stored somewhere inside his head. Naturally, Jimmy knew all the answers to all the questions Miss Gwen asked.

Whenever Miss Gwen asked a question, the answer just popped up in his head. Jimmy could have been the fastest student to give the correct answers, and he could have been noticed by everyone.

However, Jimmy never raised his hand to answer any questions, not ever! He just sat in his seat, *thinking* the answers to himself because he was very, very shy to say anything out loud.

Once, Miss Gwen tried to make Jimmy stand up and read a line from a book. Jimmy nearly fainted. He blushed all over, and his whole body shook. After that, Miss Gwen gave up asking Jimmy anything. She already knew that Jimmy was clever, and that he had all the answers in his head. Maybe that was why Jimmy had such a huge head– to store all that knowledge. His head was larger than anyone else's. It was even bigger than a basketball. Still, not many people noticed him in class, even with his large head.

But one day, there was a problem...

Chapter 2
The Writing Class

The problem started in English class. It was time for writing. Miss Gwen wrote a topic on the board and faced the class.

"The topic for today is 'Learning from Friends,'" said Miss Gwen. "We all learn something from other people. Now, let's brainstorm ideas. Who can tell me some of the things we can learn from our friends?"

All hands were raised except Jimmy's.

"I can learn to pick my nose like William. He can do it really well," said Eric with a giggle.

"I can learn to cheat on tests like Eric," said William.

"Kristy always cries, so I can learn to cry, too," said Cindy.

"Luke taught me how to touch my ear with my tongue," said Max.

While all the students were shouting out their ideas, Jimmy sat there listening and thinking. Jimmy liked brainstorming. Ideas popped up in his head and zoomed around. He concentrated on brainstorming more ideas. He concentrated and concentrated until suddenly his head hit something with a loud thud.

Jimmy looked up. He seemed to have banged his head on the wall. No. It was not the wall. It was the ceiling! Jimmy looked down. Everyone was staring up at him. They were so shocked at the sight that nobody could talk. Jimmy's large head had become larger. It had blown up like a balloon.

It was a balloon. It was floating on the ceiling,

and it was carrying Jimmy's body with it.

Everyone stared in silence until, finally,

Miss Gwen said, "What's going on?
Jimmy, are you OK?"

Jimmy was confused. He tried to move down, but he couldn't. His head was pressed against the ceiling, and his head seemed to want to fly higher. He tried to jerk his head this way and that. He waved his arms as if he was swimming. He pushed on the ceiling to move downward. Instead, Jimmy found himself flying out the open window.

Jimmy flew upward. Up, up, and up he went. He flew higher and higher into the blue sky.

Jimmy was shooting up like a hot air balloon. He passed by puzzled birds as he flew up toward the clouds. Soon, he lost sight of his school. He lost sight of the streets and the trees and the whole neighborhood.

Jimmy was afraid he might fly out into space. He thought he might be zapped into a black hole or bump into a satellite. Thankfully, that didn't happen.

18

Jimmy's head slowed down and finally stopped in the clouds. Jimmy floated in midair.

'What just happened?' thought Jimmy. 'Where am I?'

Jimmy didn't know what to do. He was surrounded by white clouds. He couldn't look down. He was afraid he might drop to the ground like a shooting star. He was too scared to cry out for help.

Suddenly, Jimmy heard a voice behind him.

"Who is that boy over there?"

Jimmy swung around to see where the voice was coming from. There were two old men sitting on a cloud playing chess! Their heads were as big as Jimmy's. Was Jimmy dreaming? Who were these old men? Were they angels?

"W... What?" Jimmy croaked.

"Hey! What are you doing here, young man?" asked one of the men with a long beard. He looked Jimmy up and down.

"I... I don't know," mumbled Jimmy. "I don't know what I'm doing here. I don't know how I got here. I just... flew up."

"Well..." the other man said, "you have obviously been brainstorming."

Jimmy looked at him, surprised. Who were these men?

"How did you know I was brainstorming?" asked Jimmy.

"I can hear the storm in your head," the bearded man said.

"Boy, isn't that noisy!" exclaimed

the other man. "What are you doing with all those brainstorm clouds in your head?"

"I don't hear anything," said Jimmy.

"Well, of course you do. Listen carefully to the sound in your head," said the bearded man, who was starting to get a little irritated.

Jimmy closed his eyes. What were these men talking about? Was something really happening inside his head? He tried to listen to the sound in his head. At first, he didn't hear anything. Then he heard a small rumbling noise from far away. *'Maybe I imagined it,'* thought Jimmy.

However, the sound grew nearer and nearer. He could clearly hear the rumbling sound of thunder. He heard the whooshing sound of the wind. He heard the rattling noise of tree branches. He heard rockets and fireworks. He heard the roaring engines of planes and helicopters. He heard loud trumpets and drums. He heard all sorts of things. **The sounds were coming from inside his head!**

Chapter 4
Storm in the Head

Jimmy looked at the old men with excitement. They looked back at Jimmy with curiosity.

"There is a storm in my head!" exclaimed Jimmy, who was starting to feel dizzy from all the noise spinning around in his head.

"Of course there is," said the bearded man, looking at Jimmy in amazement.

"You didn't know you had a storm? Everyone has one. When you start brainstorming, the storm grows in your head," said the other man.

"But everyone else was brainstorming," said Jimmy, confused. "We were all brainstorming together in the same classroom. Why am I the only one flying up here?"

The old men looked at each other and then looked at the boy carefully.

"If you didn't want to be up here, why did you keep the storm in your head?" asked the bearded man.

"I didn't keep the storm," said Jimmy.

"Of course you did. You've locked the storm in your head. You've never let the wind blow out. You've never let the planes out to fly free or the rockets to reach the moon. You've kept it all to yourself, haven't you?" said the other man.

"What do you mean?" Jimmy was getting really confused.

"You see, you have to let the storm out or the wind just gets stronger and stronger. You can let it out easily through your mouth," explained the bearded man. "I mean you have to release your ideas out of your head. If you don't talk about your ideas, your head gets bigger and bigger and it lifts you up."

"You mean my head lifted me up because I didn't talk?" asked Jimmy.

"Isn't that obvious? Your thoughts grew and grew until they formed a huge storm. The strong twister is lifting you up right now," said the other man.

"Oh, no. What should I do? How will I ever get down?" cried Jimmy.

"You have to pull your ideas out of your head. That's what everyone else does after brainstorming," said the bearded man.

"Are you brainstormers, too?" asked Jimmy.

"Of course, why else would we be up here?" the bearded man laughed as if it was a joke.

"What are you brainstorming about?" asked Jimmy.

"Do you think I'll tell you what I'm thinking about? Why would I do that?" asked the bearded man. He suddenly looked very serious. "If I tell you my ideas, I will lose the chess game and be dragged down. I don't want that."

"Don't you ever go down?" asked Jimmy.

"Only after we finish playing the chess game," replied the bearded man, shaking his head.

"We go down when we are ready to share our ideas with people," said the other man.

"Well, I want to go down now.
I want to sit in a chair and listen to my friends talk," said Jimmy.

"Then you must release the storm from your head. I think you have a long way to go, so you had better get started, young man. And please stop interrupting us," said the bearded man.

Then the old men turned to face each other. They concentrated on the chess board again. They didn't speak. They just sat there *thinking*.

Chapter 5

On the Ground Again

Jimmy had to get the storm out of his head. He had to go down to the ground. He decided to talk out loud about all the things he had learned. He recited the multiplication table. He recited the capital cities of all the countries in the world. He summarized all the storybooks that he had ever read since kindergarten. He talked and talked and talked about what he knew, what he had learned, and what he had thought about.

Suddenly, Jimmy felt someone grabbing his arm. He jerked his head up. It was Eric!

"Hey, you came down! I was really worried about you. Are you okay?" asked Eric. His eyes were full of tears.

Jimmy's classmates were standing in the playground holding Jimmy's arms.

"I thought you were going to float up into space," said William.

"I thought you were an alien," said Luke.

"I thought I could never come down," said Jimmy. But he was safely back down. He had talked all those ideas out of his head until he was all the way back down!

After that, everyone noticed Jimmy. He became the most popular boy in the whole school, not because he was clever, and not because he had flown to the sky, but because he told so many interesting stories. Everyone loved listening to Jimmy talk.

Jimmy didn't know he could talk so much, but he discovered that it was fun talking to other people. Maybe that was why Jimmy had such a huge head- to store all the stories he could tell his friends.

Not many people talked about how Jimmy had flown into the sky that day. Nobody understood how and why, so they stopped talking about it. Only, in English class, when everyone was brainstorming ideas, Miss Gwen never forgot to tie a ribbon around Jimmy's ankle, just in case.